KEVIN HENKES

A PARADE OF ELEPHANTS

Greenwillow Books • *An Imprint of* HarperCollins*Publishers*

A Parade of Elephants
Copyright © 2018 by Kevin Henkes
All rights reserved. Printed in the United States of America.
For information address HarperCollins Children's Books,
a division of HarperCollins Publishers, 195 Broadway, New York, NY 10007.
www.harpercollinschildrens.com

Brown ink and gouache were used to prepare the full-color art.
The text type is 46-point Futura Medium.

Library of Congress Cataloging-in-Publication Data

Names: Henkes, Kevin, author, illustrator.
Title: A parade of elephants / Kevin Henkes.
Description: First edition. |
New York, NY : Greenwillow Books, an imprint of HarperCollins Publishers, [2018] |
Summary: Illustrations and easy-to-read text introduce such basic concepts
as adjectives, adverbs, daytime, and nighttime as they follow five elephants
marching from dawn to dusk.
Identifiers: LCCN 2018025850 | ISBN 9780062668271 (hardback) |
ISBN 9780062668288 (lib. bdg.)
Subjects: | CYAC: Elephants—Fiction. | BISAC: JUVENILE FICTION / Animals / Elephants. |
JUVENILE FICTION / Imagination & Play. | JUVENILE FICTION / Concepts / General.
Classification: LCC PZ7.H389 Par 2018 | DDC [E]—dc23
LC record available at https://lccn.loc.gov/2018025850

18 19 20 21 22 WOR 10 9 8 7 6 5 4 3 2 1
First Edition

Greenwillow Books

To SCH & VAD
From KJH

Look!

Elephants!

One,	
two,	
three,	
four,	
five.	

Five elephants.

Marching.

A parade of elephants!

Big and round
and round they are.
Big and round
and round they go.

Up, down.

Over, under.

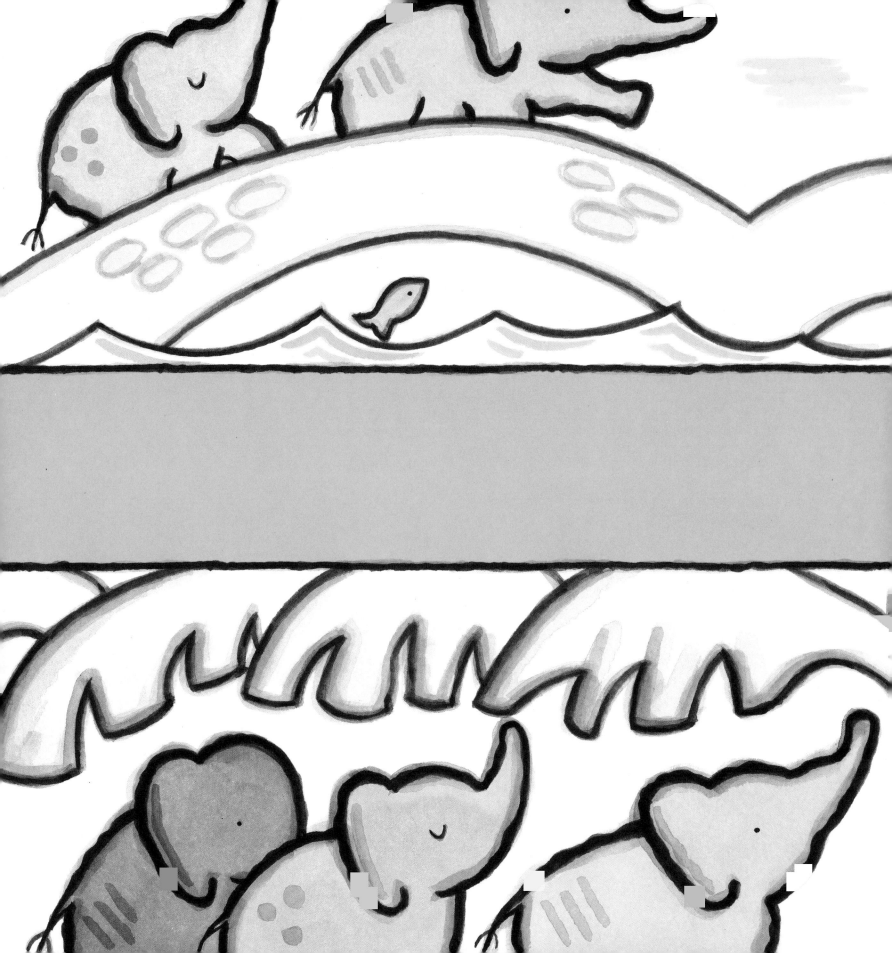

In, out.

They march

and they march

and they march.

They

march

all

day.

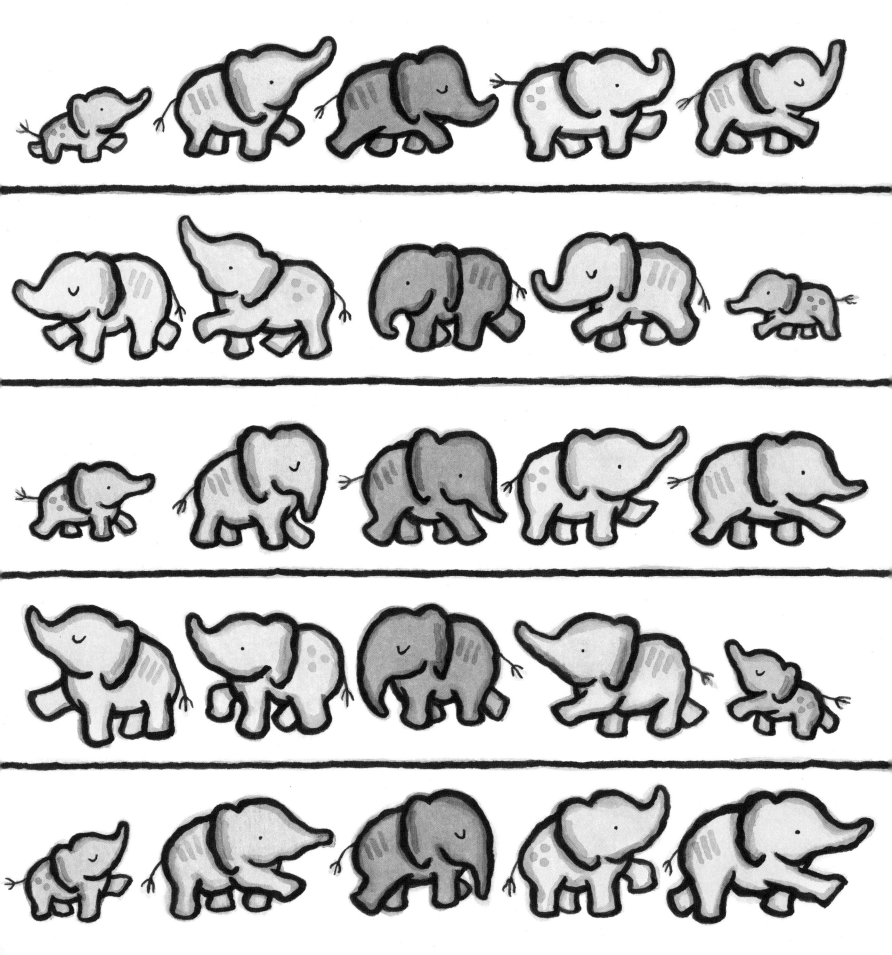

And when the day is done,

they are done, too.

They yawn and stretch.

They stretch and yawn.

But before they sleep

they lift their trunks . . .

and they trumpet—

scattering stars across the sky.

Good night.